To the bravest person I know. My sister, Sara.

First Edition
ISBN: 978-1-5324-0192-3
eISBN: 978-1-5324-0193-0
Published in the United States by Xist Publishing
www.xistpublishing.com
PO Box 61593 Irvine, CA 92602

The Sad Sad Monster

Dolores Costello

This is a story about
a monster.

A very good monster.

But even though he was good, everyone was afraid of him.

At school, nobody would
play with him.

He would swing alone.

Skip alone.

And play games alone.

So Monster was sad.
Very sad.

One day, Monster
was eating lunch.

Everyone sat somewhere else.
Everyone except Sarah.

Sarah wasn't afraid. She didn't mind Monster's sharp teeth.

She very much
wanted to swing
with Monster.

And Skip.

And play games.

Sarah wanted to be
Monster's friend.

After that, Monster
wasn't sad or
alone anymore.

74338645R00020

Made in the USA
Middletown, DE
23 May 2018